# DINOTRUX

## MEET GARBY!

Adapted by
Margaret Green

## L B

**LITTLE, BROWN AND COMPANY**
New York   Boston

DREAMWORKS

DINOTRUX

Attention, DINOTRUX fans!
Look for these words
when you read this book.
Can you spot them all?

Revvit

Garby

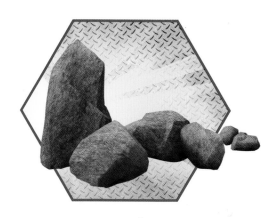

rock

D-Structs

The Dinotrux were eating ore
for breakfast.
Ty stopped chewing.
"Does this taste funny?" he asked.

"Stop eating!" Revvit said.

"There is tar on all the ore!"

D-Structs had played a mean trick.

He put tar on the ore!

"We need to build a safe station
to store our ore," Ty said.
Revvit drew up a plan.

"We should build it with a
super-strong kind of rock
so D-Structs cannot smash it,"
Ty said.

A Stegarbasaurus could help.

A Stegarbasaurus eats rocks.

But when Ty and Revvit drove up,

all the Stegarbasauruses raced off!

All except one.
"Are you the T-Trux
who took on D-Structs?"
the Stegarbasaurus asked.

Ty introduced himself and Revvit.
"My name is Garby,"
said the Stegarbasaurus.

"That is a tiny tool!"

Garby said about Revvit.

Revvit frowned.

Garby agreed to help.

"I know the perfect kind of rock!"

he said.

He and Revvit went off to find it.

Garby pointed to the special rock.
"This will do the job," he said.

"Thank you for your help," Revvit said.

Garby saw a rock to chomp.

He did not see Revvit next to the rock.

He chomped the rock,

and chomped Revvit, too!

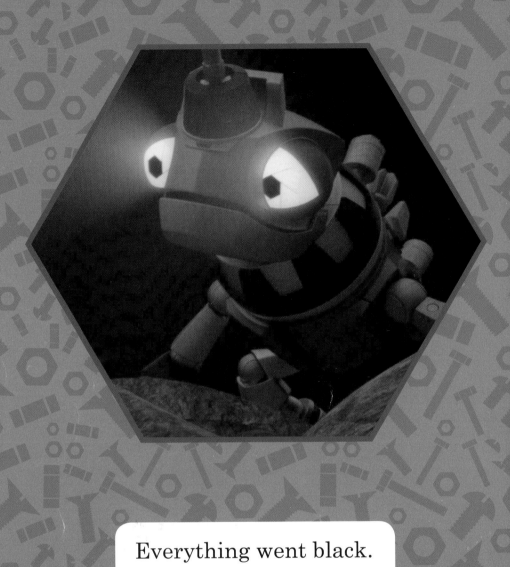

Everything went black.
Revvit realized that
he was inside Garby!

The tools in his stomach
began to crush rocks.
Revvit snuck past before
they could crush him, too.

Outside, Garby found the
other Dinotrux.
"Where is Revvit?"
they asked.

"Maybe D-Structs got him,"
said Garby.

"It is time to take this battle to D-Structs," Ty said.

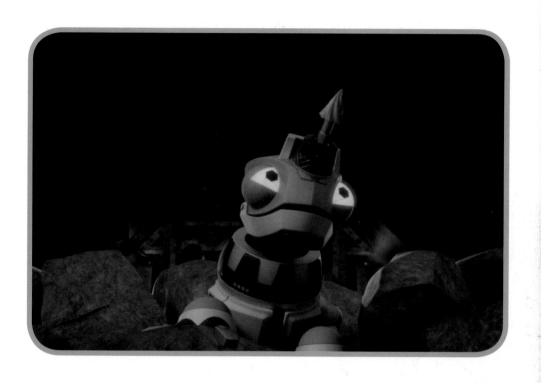

"Uh-oh!" said Revvit
from inside Garby.

"Where is Revvit?"
Ty asked D-Structs.
"Why would I know?"
he answered.

Just then, a brick popped out of Garby.

Revvit was inside the brick!

The Trux were happy
to have Revvit back.
But then D-Structs smashed
a pile of rocks to trap them!

"Do not worry!" said Garby.
He ate the rocks
and freed the Dinotrux.

D-Structs was headed
to destroy their garage.

The Dinotrux caught up.
Garby shot spikes and
bricks at D-Structs
until the T-Trux drove off.

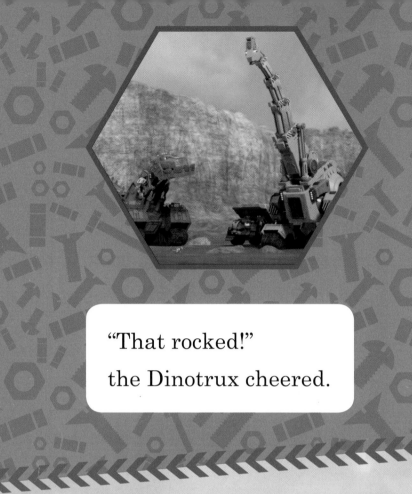

"That rocked!"
the Dinotrux cheered.

"And now I know just
what rocks to use,"
Revvit said.

Garby helped the Dinotrux
build a strong ore station.
"Let D-Structs try to mess
with that!" said Ty.